William Shakespeare

Much Ado About Nothing

Retold by
Marcia Williams

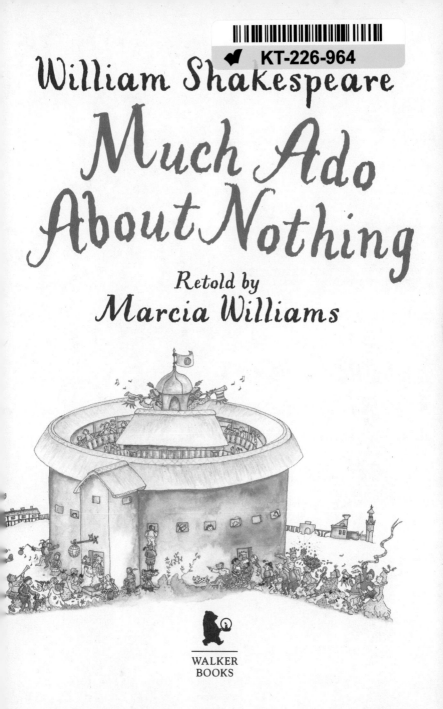

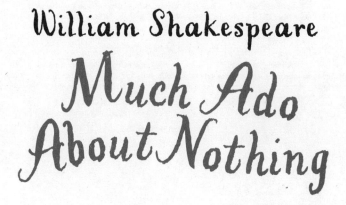

William Shakespeare

Much Ado About Nothing

First published 2015 by Walker Books Ltd
87 Vauxhall Walk, London SE11 5HJ

2 4 6 8 10 9 7 5 3 1

© 2000, 2014 Marcia Williams

The right of Marcia Williams to be identified as author/illustrator of this work
has been asserted by her in accordance with the Copyright, Designs and Patents Act 1988

This book has been typeset in Kennerly Regular

Printed and bound in Germany

British Library Cataloguing in Publication Data:
a catalogue record for this book is available from the British Library

ISBN 978-1-4063-6278-7

www.walker.co.uk

For Ruby

Contents

In which a love
match is made.

There was such a bustle of excitement
at the governor's house in Messina,
Sicily. The governor, Leonato, had just
received word that guests were about
to arrive – and not just any guests! Don
Pedro, the Prince of Aragon, was coming
with his brother Don John and two
handsome young officers – Claudio, a
lord of Florence, and Benedick, a lord of

Padua. The last time they had visited, they were about to go to war. Now they were returning after a successful campaign and would have time for fun. All the gentlemen arrived dressed to please the ladies – all, that is, except for Seignior Benedick. He was a soldier through and through, so he wore his uniform and his face remained unshaven. Besides, he had no time for ladies and had sworn never to marry.

Leonato had a very sweet daughter called Hero and a beautiful niece called Beatrice. Hero was as charming and good tempered as a summer's day, and Beatrice was as sparky and vivid as an autumn storm! Since the gentlemen's last visit, Hero had secretly held a spot in her heart for Seignior Claudio, but

Beatrice had no time for men. She found Seignior Benedick particularly annoying and had swapped sharp words with him on every previous visit. It seemed that this occasion was to be no different.

"What! My dear Lady Disdain, Are you yet living?" said Benedick.

"Is it possible Disdain should die, while she hath such meet food to feed it as Seignior Benedick?" countered Beatrice.

The greeting between Hero and Claudio went very differently, for although not a

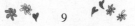

word passed between them, Claudio could not take his eyes off the lady. He felt himself being captured by her gentle innocence and he could hardly wait to discuss the matter with Benedick.

"Benedick, didst thou note the daughter of Seignior Leonato?" he burst out. "In mine eye she is the sweetest lady that I ever looked on."

"I can see yet without spectacles and I see no such matter," replied his friend.

Don Pedro, on the other hand, was a true

romantic and was delighted to hear that Claudio had fallen in love with such a suitable young lady. He promised to further Claudio's suit at the masked ball to be held that very evening.

Then Don Pedro turned to Benedick, who was noisily declaring he would live and die a bachelor. "I shall see thee, ere I die, look pale with love," promised Don Pedro.

"With anger, with sickness, or with hunger, my lord, not with love!" Benedick assured him.

Later that night, amidst the merry music and dancing, Benedick and Beatrice continued their sparring. Hero, on the other hand, had only soft words to speak to her Claudio, and before the evening ended Don Pedro had gained her father's consent to a marriage. Claudio was speechless with gratitude and delight!

"Speak, Count, 'tis your cue," laughed Beatrice.

"Silence is the perfectest herald of joy," cried Claudio, eventually finding his voice. "I were but a little happy, if I could say how much."

"Good Lord, for alliance! Thus goes everyone to the world but I," said Beatrice, with an unconvincing sigh. "I may sit in the corner and cry heigh-ho for a husband!"

With that, the lady vanished into the night, leaving Don Pedro wondering, just wondering, if having managed one love match, he might not arrange another... "She were an excellent wife for Benedick," he announced, delighted with the thought.

"Oh lord!" exclaimed Leonato in horror. "My lord, if they were but a week married, they would talk themselves mad!"

However, Don Pedro was not to be dissuaded. "I will bring Seignior Benedick

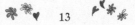

and the lady Beatrice into a mountain of affection the one with the other," he promised. Claudio, Hero and Leonato agreed to help him, even though they thought it a mad idea with not a chance of success. For no two people were more eager to stay single than Beatrice and Benedick.

In which a plan unfolds.

The following day, the three conspirators set about their task. As Benedick was resting alone in the arbour in Leonato's garden, Don Pedro, Claudio and Leonato passed close by. Benedick just happened to overhear them say that Beatrice was sick with love for him.

"What was it you told me of today, that your niece Beatrice was in love with

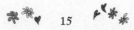

Seignior Benedick?" said Don Pedro casually,
if a touch too loudly.

"She loves him with an enraged affection,"
declared the count.

"Tears her hair, prays, curses, O sweet
Benedick!" said Claudio.

Benedick was most amazed. To begin with
he thought it must be some trick, but then he
felt convinced that Leonato would not lie.

This can be no trick, he thought. "Love me!
It must be requited! When I said I would die
a bachelor, I did not think I should live till
I was married," he informed the birds that
flapped around the arbour.

So the conspirators had hooked their
first fish! Benedick had believed them. He
resolved to give up being proud and love
Beatrice back.

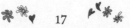

Later that same morning, Beatrice was
resting alone in the arbour in Leonato's
garden when Hero and her maid, Ursula,
passed close by. Beatrice just happened to
overhear them say that Benedick was sick
with love for her.

"But are you sure that Benedick loves

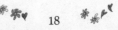

Beatrice so entirely?" Ursula quizzed her
mistress.

"So says the prince and my new-trothed
lord," declared Hero, in her most innocent
voice.

Beatrice was amazed – almost more
amazed than Benedick had been to hear

that she loved him. "What fire is in mine ears?" she wondered. "Can this be true?" Yet Beatrice felt convinced that her sweet cousin would not lie. She would have to believe her friends. In an instant, she resolved to give up being haughty and return Benedick's love. "Contempt, farewell! And, Benedick, love on; I will requite thee," she cried.

In which we meet a meddlesome pair.

Meanwhile, Don Pedro's spiteful brother Don John and his cohort Borachio were plotting to ruin Hero's wedding plans. Don John hated his brother and would do anything to upset him. So when he heard that Don Pedro had arranged the wedding of Claudio and Hero for the following day, he vowed to destroy the happy event.

"It is so; the count Claudio shall marry

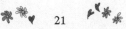

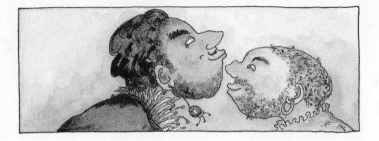

the daughter of Leonato?" he asked
Borachio.

"Yea, my lord; but I can cross it," Borachio
replied with a sneer.

Don John smiled at the thought. He
handed Borachio a large sum of money. Then
he listened eagerly to Borachio's plan and
shook Borachio warmly by the hand.

Later that night, Don John persuaded
Don Pedro and Claudio to stand under
one of the upstairs windows of Leonato's
house. Standing hidden in the shadows,

they looked up and saw they were below
Hero's bedroom – and then they thought
they saw Hero embrace Borachio and
whisper in his ear. Claudio could not
believe his eyes: surely his sweet Hero
would not behave in such a terrible,
disloyal way? Yet he could not deny the
evidence of his own eyes.

At first he was numb with shock, but
then he felt foolish for believing her sweet,
innocent looks and he was overcome with
anger and hatred for her. He decided to

show the whole household what a deceiving
minx Hero was.

In which a wedding is called off.

The following day, an excited party gathered inside the local church to celebrate the wedding of Claudio and Hero. Hero smiled happily as she joined Claudio at the altar – but just as Friar Francis was about to marry them, Claudio turned on Hero and accused her of disloyalty.

A gasp ran round the chapel. How could this be? Leonato's lovely daughter? Yet

Claudio was not to be checked.

"Give not this rotten orange to your friend," he shouted at Leonato. "She's but a sign and semblance of her honour."

"Is my lord well, that he doth speak so wide?" cried Hero.

"What do you mean, my lord?" cried Leonato, astonished and hurt that his daughter should be slandered in this way. However, when Don Pedro also bore witness against Hero, even her own father began to believe the terrible accusation.

Overcome by shock and heartache, Hero fell to the ground in a deathlike trance.

"How doth the lady?" asked Benedick.

"Dead I think! Help, uncle! Hero, uncle, Seignior Benedick, Friar!" cried Beatrice in rising panic.

As the wedding guests left the church, Hero's colour gradually returned and her eyes opened. The friar, who knew Hero would never have committed such a sin, thought her faint might be used to advantage. "Let her awhile be secretly kept in," he said, "and publish it that she is dead indeed." He hoped that the false news of her death might knock some sense into Claudio.

In which the lies are revealed.

Meanwhile, shocked and upset that her cousin had been slandered in such a manner, Beatrice could not stop her tears. When Benedick saw this, he was overcome with pity for her. Suddenly, he could control himself no longer and blurted out his love for her.

"I do love nothing in the world so well as you: is not that strange," he said, waiting to be rebuffed.

"I love you with so much of my heart that none is left to protest," came the unexpected answer.

On a cloud of happiness, Benedick asked Beatrice to bid him do anything to prove his love and to stem her tears, but he was horrified by Beatrice's chill request:

"Kill Claudio."

"Ha! Not for the wide world," cried Benedick.

"You kill me

to deny it," said Beatrice. "Farewell."

Benedick could not bear to lose Beatrice's love so

soon after winning it, so after much persuasion he agreed to fight his friend.

Luckily for Benedick, before the fight could take place, Borachio was heard by the night watch talking about his conspiracy with Don John. "Therefore know, I have earned

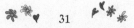

of Don John a thousand ducats," Borachio
boasted.

Borachio was arrested and forced to
confess to Don Pedro. "Don John your brother
incensed me to slander the lady Hero, and
paid me richly for the practice of it," Borachio
admitted. Poor Don Pedro was horrified
when he heard that the woman he had seen
embracing Borachio was not Hero, but a maid
Borachio had tricked into wearing Hero's
clothes. When he learned that his brother,

Don John, had run away, he knew for sure
that he and Claudio had been duped.

Claudio was filled with remorse for
having, as he believed, caused sweet Hero's
death. "Impose me to what penance your
invention can lay upon my sin," he begged.

"I cannot bid you bid my daughter live," said Leonato, feigning a broken heart.

Leonato instructed Claudio instead to spend the night beside Hero's tomb, singing of her innocence, and to go back to the church the following morning and marry Hero's cousin, whom he did not know. Claudio was so filled with shame that he

was prepared to agree to anything. So that
night he made his way to a tomb prepared
for Hero, and spent the night in tears and
song.

In which a wedding
takes place.

As morning broke and the wedding bells
rang out, Claudio made his way to church.

His heart was heavy, but he was determined to take his punishment and marry Hero's cousin, even if she was as ugly and bristly as a broom. Two ladies arrived and walked down the aisle towards him, hidden behind masks.

"Are you yet determin'd today to marry with my brother's daughter?" asked Leonato.

"I'll hold my mind." replied Claudio. "Which is the lady I must seize upon?"

"This same is she, and I do give you to her," replied Leonato's brother, Antonio.

The first lady removed her mask – but she was not Hero's unknown cousin. She was Hero herself! Claudio was overcome with amazement. "Another Hero!" he cried.

"Nothing certainer," smiled Hero. "One Hero died defil'd, but I do live!"

"The former Hero!" exclaimed Don Pedro

in delight. "Hero that is dead!"

"She died, my lord, but whiles her slander
liv'd," answered Leonato.

Then everyone turned as the second lady
removed her mask. There stood Beatrice,
looking every inch the modest bride, but still
bent on teasing her beloved Benedick.

"Do not you love me?" asked Benedick
hopefully.

"Why, no," she replied, "no more than reason."

"Come, cousin," laughed Leonato, "I am sure you love the gentleman."

"And I'll be sworn upon't that he loves her," declared Claudio.

After much playful banter between Beatrice and Benedick, which Benedick

finally managed to put a stop to with a kiss,

Beatrice and Benedick agreed to wed.

Friar Francis and all the reassembled
guests cheered with delight, for all believed

that the couples were perfectly matched. Without further ado, Friar Francis united them in matrimony. Even Beatrice and Benedick, who had so scorned marriage, seemed overcome with joy.

When news arrived that Don John had been captured, the wedding party decided to think of a punishment for him another time. They revelled in their happiness, and feasted and danced through the sun-filled day and the sweet-scented Sicilian night!

WILLIAM SHAKESPEARE was a popular playwright, poet and actor who lived in Elizabethan England. He married in Stratford-upon-Avon aged eighteen and had three children, although one died in childhood. Shakespeare then moved to London, where he wrote 39 plays and over 150 sonnets, many of which are still very popular today. In fact, his plays are performed more often than those of any other playwright, and he died 450 years ago! His gravestone includes a curse against interfering with his burial place, possibly to

deter people from opening it in search of unpublished manuscripts. It reads, "Blessed be the man that spares these stones, and cursed be he that moves my bones." Spooky!

 **MARCIA WILLIAMS'** mother was a novelist and her father a playwright, so it's not surprising that Marcia ended up an author herself. Although she never trained formally as an artist, she found that motherhood, and the time she spent later as a nursery school teacher, inspired her to start writing and illustrating children's books.

Marcia's books bring to life some of the world's all-time favourite stories and some colourful historical characters. Her hilarious retellings and clever observations will have children laughing out loud and coming back for more!

More retellings from Marcia Williams

Charles Dickens'
OLIVER TWIST
Retold and Illustrated by
Marcia Williams

ISBN 978-1-4063-5692-2

Charles Dickens'
GREAT
EXPECTATIONS
Retold and Illustrated by
Marcia Williams

ISBN 978-1-4063-5693-9

Charles Dickens'
A CHRISTMAS
CAROL
Retold and Illustrated by
Marcia Williams

ISBN 978-1-4063-5694-6

Charles Dickens'
DAVID
COPPERFIELD
Retold and Illustrated by
Marcia Williams

ISBN 978-1-4063-5695-3

Available from all good booksellers

www.walker.co.uk